Blood Ties

Karen J Carlisle

An original James Findlay Journals Adventure

Kraken Publishing

Blood Ties
An original James Findlay Journal #1

A catalogue record for this book is available from the National Library of Australia

Also available separately as eBook.

This book is written in British English.
Printed in Australia.

Typeset in Times Roman 12pt.

Published by Kraken Publishing.
www.krakenpublishing.com
www. karenjcarlisle.com

For my readers who insisted I continue
James Findlay's journey,
for my family who stood by me,
and because my need to understand the darker side
of humanity will never cease.

Contents

Introduction

Welcome Gentle Reader, to the first instalment of the *Journals of James Findlay* (also known as 'Jack the Ripper' and 'Doctor Jack'). *Blood Ties* is a mini-adventure, continuing James' story directly after he boarded a ship to places unknown, in the novella *Doctor Jack*, the novella in the first book of my Victorian steampunk mystery series *The Adventures of Viola Stewart*. *Doctor Jack* was originally written and published in 2015,

For those who haven't read *Doctor Jack*, I've added the scene mentioned above: the last scene in which we see James/Jack. It is written from his point of view.

Prologue

Excerpt from *Doctor Jack*: *The Adventures of Viola Stewart*

Jack pulled up the collar of his thick wool coat then tugged down the sleeves, ensuring his wrists were covered. He tapped his new bowler so that it sat low on his brow, and ran his finger along the silver thread of the red feather that was tucked neatly in its band.

The sky was clear, allowing the fog to seep between the dockyard buildings. He slipped easily through the gloom, unseen by prying eyes as he hurried to his rendezvous. He chuckled as he jumped a large puddle, landing on the edge of the footpath.

Trolley wheels clattered and bounced on the cobble stones behind him, as his valet grumbled and struggled to keep up. The luggage-laden trolley jolted to an abrupt halt as it hit the gutter. The valet groaned. He leaned into the trolley and edged it up onto the footpath, then kicked one of the wheels back into alignment.

Jack's grin widened.

"Keep up!"

Jack heard muffled voices as they neared the dock. He slowed his pace, motioning for the valet to halt.

"Stay here," he demanded, "and not a word."

Jack edged closer, cocking his ear towards the conversation. The voices were faint, hidden somewhere ahead in the maze of old buildings and fog. He moved onward towards them.

"There's always a problem when a wild dog gets the taste for blood. It either has to be sent away or be put down." Jack recognised the voice of Mr Browne.

"What fate has The Society pronounced for him?" asked his co-conspirator.

"We have invested much in him, Mr Grey." There was a pause, then Mr Browne continued. "But it will depend on his next step."

Mr Grey scoffed. "Do you think they can control him?"

"The Society can control everyone. Eventually," said Mr Browne.

"And when we have them, they are ours for life." Mr Grey chuckled.

"As long as they are of use," replied Mr Browne.

Mr Grey cleared his throat.

Jack stepped into the cramped courtyard. Talons of fog clawed at his woollen coat, unwilling to abandon him. His footsteps rang loudly on the cobblestones.

"Good evening, Jack," said Mr Browne. "Excellent timing, as usual."

Jack nodded.

"Glad you could join us," Mr Browne swept his arm in the direction of his associate. "You have met Mr Grey?"

"Ah yes. Mr Grey was kind enough to supply an alibi for my time in Marylebone," said Jack, extending his left hand in greeting.

Mr Browne took an expeditious step away from Mr Grey.

The ring of metal echoed loudly in the murky courtyard, as Jack's blade slid from its holster to greet Mr Grey. He groaned and grabbed his stomach. His eyes widened. A furrow deepened on his forehead as his eyebrows wrinkled. Water welled in his eyes. He turned to Mr Browne. His knees betrayed him.

"Why?" he gasped.

"Because you belong to us and, now you are known to The Metropolitan Police Force, you have become a liability. Abberline has been looking for you."

Mr Browne plucked his fob watch from his waistcoat pocket and flicked it open.

"The ship will be sailing soon, Jack. Best not miss it." He snapped the cover shut and turned his back on Mr Grey.

Jack stooped down and, with a quick flick, ended Mr Grey's pain.

He picked up Mr Grey's bowler, dusted it off and handed it to Mr Browne.

"You can smell the sea from here," said Mr Browne. He took a deep breath then slowly exhaled.

"And dog shit," said Jack, as he handed Mr Grey's hat to Mr Browne. "And where is your new lapdog?"

"Awaiting my command," replied Mr Browne.

Blood Ties

New Ground

High tide lapped the steamship's hull. Lamplight flared in the evening fog, making it difficult to manoeuvre through the throng of well-wishers waving off their loved ones.

The ramp knocked against the wooden deck as Jack Findlay boarded the steamship. It was touted as the fastest ship to journey London to Adelaide. The faster, the better. He tugged his collar up against the evening chill. He was used to the city, and the anonymity of its dark alleys and winding Underground.

He glanced at the water swelling beneath the ramp. He wasn't fond of open water. Less so when he was imprisoned in a metal coffin bobbing across said open water. People became too familiar in such confined spaces.

"Good evening, sir." The steward nodded in greeting. His white-gloved fingers curled around the handle of Jack's leather valise.

The metal joints on Jack's mechanical hand clicked inside

his own glove as he tugged it away from the steward.

"No," he grumbled.

The steward snapped to attention and avoided Jack's glare.

Jack cleared his throat. "It's my..." He held the valise against his chest. "Tools of my profession."

Jack stared at the steward and smiled. He'd discovered people found it disturbing to look him in the eye.

"My apologies, Mr...?" The steward took a step back, still avoiding direct eye contact.

Jack wanted to reply: I am Jack Findlay, the notorious Ripper. He was proud of who he was, what he'd achieved. He was so close to completing his research. To be sent abroad just when things were getting interesting...

He clenched his teeth and tugged his left coat cuff down over his glove. He couldn't give his own name; the authorities were most likely looking for Jack Findlay. He required an alias - one that would engender trust.

He smiled. "Dr Collins," he replied, "retired police surgeon."

"Welcome aboard, Doctor Collins. I'm Mr. Cox, here to ensure you enjoy your journey with us."

The ship's horn howled through the fog.

The chatter of excited passengers engulfed him, as they milled around the edge of the deck and leaned over the ship's rail. Squawking children darted through the confusion of starched suits and skirts festooned with bows and ruffled passementerie.

Jack sneered. It was all too disorderly.

The ship's engines rumbled below his feet. Deck lamps flickered gently in the breeze. The paddle wheel housing cast a shadow across the deck.

Jack sidestepped the crush and gravitated towards the security of the darkness, away from the waving passengers. Sails slapped against their masts as the wind picked up.

The ship's horn mourned slowly, as if it knew of his plans for the voyage.

A light tube crackled on the wall near the cabin door. Its pale blue light reflected in the polished brass fittings and danced on the wood panelled walls.

A bottle of champagne and a full crystal champagne flute, bubbles still popping at the surface, stood on the table next to a padded leather settee.

Jack ignored the invitation; there would be time to celebrate after his work was complete. He removed his bowler and dusted droplets of moisture from the red feather sewn into the hatband. He would miss England; he'd found great sport there.

A cool breeze lifted the curtains, revealing the etched glass of the open porthole. There was a faint splash. And another. The ship's engine thrummed under his feet. A rush of bubbles broke the surface of the champagne. The splashes became rhythmic, like the tick tock of a clock.

Jack peered through the porthole as the steamship made its way out of the harbour. London was adrift in the night fog.

He placed his hat on the table by the untouched champagne and surveyed the cabin suite's sitting room. A green padded-leather settee stood next to the table along the closest wall. A small dining table, with a pressed, lace-edged linen cloth, and matching chairs sat in the centre of the room. Candelabras were positioned at each end of a side table on the far wall. Jack's steamer trunk sat, still unopened, just inside the doorway to the adjoining room.

Knocking noises emanated from the other side of the wall.

Jack's mechanical hand twitched; its gears whirred. He snatched up his new walking cane and waited.

A ginger-haired man in a dark grey suit emerged from the sleeping quarters.

Jack's muscles relaxed. He tugged off his left glove and flexed the joints of the metal fingers.

"You've arrived, sir?" Evans wiped dark smudges from his hands with a rag.

"The cabin door locks?" Jack slipped off the remaining glove.

"All changed, sir," replied Evans. "The new latchkey is on the table by the bed."

"And my laboratory?"

"I don't think much of your employer's mechanics." Evans clicked his tongue. "I've had to add our own Stability Rectifier to modify the stabilising platform."

Jack strode into the private sleeping quarters.

The bed had been relocated to one side. In its place was a raised platform suspended in a low, metal cradle. On it were a workbench and carved wooden chair. A large wooden trunk, bound with padlocked metal straps, stood under the window.

Jack smiled; his employers had kept their bargain.

"Shall I set up the equipment, sir?" asked Evans.

Jack shook his head. "I prefer to do it myself."

"Very well. I'll unpack your clothes, sir." Evans shoved

the cleaning rag into his pocket.

Jack laid his right hand on Evans' forearm and studied the traces of oil ingrained around Evans' fingernails.

"Wash your hands first," he said.

"Of course, sir."

Jack waited until the door to the sitting room clicked shut, then pushed a small button at the top of his walking cane. Its head rose slowly, revealing a hidden compartment. He retrieved the trunk key from its hiding place, unlocked the padlocks and eased open the front of the trunk.

A series of drawers lined each side. A rectangular object, wrapped in waterproof cloth, fitted snugly into a niche at the bottom.

He opened one of the drawers. It caught on the runners. Something rattled inside. He eased the drawer out all the way.

It was lined with padded leather, with indentations shaped to fit glass tubes and flasks. One tube had dislodged from its recess.

He ran a flesh finger along the glass, and turned it slowly. It seemed intact. He checked each in turn. They'd all survived. He slid out the next drawer and examined its contents: various clamps and suspension rods. All intact. Evans had done an excellent job at securing his equipment.

Jack held his breath as he removed a small wooden box from the bottom drawer and placed it on the workbench. Inside was a square, metal device, with a brass plate screwed to the top and a crank on one side, and a switch on the other.

He unscrewed the plate, unlatched the lid and inspected the contents: a series of cogs and pulleys attached to the central rod, piercing the metal plate. The workings seemed to be undamaged.

He let out a long, slow breath and cranked the handle four times. The cogs quivered and whirred. Thin metal link-chains turned. The central rod turned slowly.

His eyes widened. Well done, Evans; the mixing mechanical would free up his time for more important tasks. He settled in the chair and watched. The rod turned round and round, mesmerising him with its smooth movement.

A knock on the adjoining door broke his concentration.

"Excuse me, sir." Evans opened the door. "Your dinner suit, sir."

Jack checked his pocket watch; he'd been staring at the contraption for twenty-three minutes.

"How long before the device needs resetting?" he asked.

"Fifteen minutes per revolution," replied Evans.

"And the maximum limit?"

"Two hours, sir."

Jack raised an eyebrow; Evans was proving to be a very worthwhile investment. He flipped the switch on the side of the device. The cogs froze mid-turn. The links of the metal chain clicked in place.

"Is everything satisfactory?" asked Evans.

Jack nodded.

"Will you need me for anything else, sir?"

"That will be all, Evans." Jack glanced at the wrapped box nestled in its niche at the bottom of the trunk. He just needed to collect fresh samples once they were at sea.

Desires

Small clouds of steam issued from the bottom of oval service trolleys, as they trundled across the carpet. Waiters directed them toward the occupied dining tables, removed used soup bowls and replaced them with silver cloche-covered platters. Drinks waiters filed past the tables with bottles of wine and champagne.

A pianist played a soft melody on the opposite side of the room.

Jack sat at a corner table, with his back to the wall. The full moon was barely visible through the rain droplets dribbling down the windows on the opposite wall. Hints of green and red flickered in the leadlight surround. A tube light crackled behind him, casting shadows across the crisp, white tablecloth and glinting off his silver-headed walking cane leaning against the red wallpaper, always within reach.

A young gentleman, dressed in an expensive dinner suit, sat at a nearby table, and fussed over an elegant, older woman; the man's gaze lingered on the diamond choker circling her throat.

A well-dressed couple sat at the table closest to Jack.

"The lights are faulty in our cabin." The gentleman scowled as the waiter poured his wine. "And the ones in the corridor keep fizzling out."

"I'm sorry, sir," replied their waiter. "I'll have the engineer see to it, sir. Your cabin number?"

"Mr. and Mrs. Ivers. Cabin 12B."

"I'll inform the steward you require a lamp, sir."

The waiter bowed his head and excused himself.

Mr. Ivers unfolded his napkin.

"How am I expected to see the contents of my dressing room?" Mrs. Ivers sipped her wine. "I shall have dinner in our cabin until it's fixed."

"You always look immaculate, my dear." Mr. Ivers patted his wife's gloved hand.

As if on cue, the tube lights buzzed and dimmed.

"Mark my words, Edith, this new-fangled technology won't last the voyage." He dropped his napkin on his lap.

The headwaiter paused by Jack's table. "The Captain would like to extend his welcome, Doctor Collins."

Jack smiled.

Wine glasses clinked. The ship swayed. A food trolley rolled into a table near the Dining Room entrance.

The headwaiter glanced up. More passengers had arrived for dinner. A striking woman in a magnificent emerald gown stood at the front of the crowd. She watched the drinks waiter fumble along the side of the mechanical's motor, as he struggled to extricate the trolley from the table.

She smiled and lifted her fan to her lips.

The headwaiter excused himself and strode towards the entrance.

"I do apologise for the inconvenience, Lady Ambrose. Let me escort you to your table." He retrieved a candelabra from the piano, led her past Jack, and placed the candelabra on her table.

"French champagne for Lady Ambrose." He waved the drinks waiter closer.

Flickering candlelight caught auburn highlights in her dark hair, as she swept her silk skirts to one side and settled into her chair.

Jack stared into her pale eyes. Those eyes... They reminded him of...

He took a deep breath.

Another time. Another life.

Lady Ambrose looked in his direction and smiled. Her eyes glinted green. Green, like...

Jack lifted his steaming teacup to his lips. Catherine was gone. And he was bound for a new life in the Colonies. He swallowed the liquid, scalding his tongue. He deserved it.

Lady Ambrose's gaze flickered over the room and settled on the young, well-dressed man at a nearby table.

"Who's that?" she whispered to the headwaiter.

"Lord Hubert Sebastian," he replied.

She licked her lips, eyed him over the top of her glass and slowly sipped her champagne.

Jack swallowed another mouthful of tea and set his cup down. She was so like Catherine. He longed to stay, to hold onto the memory.

Perhaps he should order dessert? Any excuse to linger longer.

His mechanical hand twitched. He had work to do; he had to collect his first sample before the first-class passengers retired for the evening, and the staff swarmed over the ship to prepare for the morning activities.

He finished his meal, dabbed his moustache with his napkin and retrieved his cane.

The Hunt

Flickering light spilled down the staircase and into First Class. Jack paused on the lower step and peered along the empty passage into the darkness.

He grinned. Evans had done his job; the tube lighting was extinguished. He was proving an excellent choice for an assistant.

Jack pulled his top hat low and turned up his jacket collar. If he was observed, he would claim he was going for a stroll on the deck.

He fished out a small disc from his pocket and tapped the device. It sprang open, unfolding into a funnel shape. He placed it on the first cabin door, and listened.

Silence.

He made his way along the passage, listening at each cabin door until he heard a faint noise from within. Something scraped inside.

He required only one subject and no witnesses. He adjusted the listening device and waited for any sign of conversation.

No voices.

Footsteps moved toward the cabin door.

Jack snapped shut the listening device, slipped it into his coat pocket, and spun on his heel to face the cabin door on the opposite side of the passage.

His mechanical hand gripped the head of his walking cane. The other wrapped around the doorknob.

The other cabin door clicked open behind him.

Jack pretended to close his adopted door, and turned to face the potential subject: a young woman, slender, sensibly dressed and, most importantly, she seemed in excellent health.

She slipped the door key into her apron pocket and hesitated.

"I'm sorry, sir." She lowered her gaze.

"No need." Jack slipped his right hand into his pocket. His fingers brushed against the cigarillo case in his pocket. He smiled, extracted the case and flicked it open.

"Don't tell the wife you saw me. I promised I'd given up." He tapped out a cigarillo. "You don't have any matches, do you?"

He popped it in his mouth and waited. It was a risky move but worth a try; being the first night onboard, it was unlikely anyone would recognise their fellow passengers yet.

The young woman reached into her apron pocket and retrieved a box of matches. She struck one, stepped closer and held it to Jack's cigarillo.

Not close enough.

His mechanical hand twitched.

He sucked in a deep breath, filling his lungs with smoke and glanced over her shoulder into the darkness. He couldn't risk anyone wandering down from dinner. It wouldn't do to alert the crew so soon in the voyage.

He needed privacy. He clenched his fingers.

Patience.

He slowly exhaled.

The maid's eyelids flickered. She inhaled and eyed the other cigarillos in the silver case.

Jack took another breath and smiled. He recognised the look of a fellow addict. He'd seen it staring back at him in the mirror. But his addiction wasn't for tobacco.

"Would you like one?" he asked.

"Well..." The maid glanced along the passage. "The Parsons have only just gone to dinner," she whispered.

"Then I won't tell," he whispered back. "I was on my way to the Promenade Deck for some fresh air. Would you care to join me?"

She bit her lip.

Just another nudge and he'd have her. He shook his cigarillo case. Her breaths quickened.

"I promise we'll be finished before they return from dinner," he said.

She nodded. "Just a quick one."

The nearby cabins were still in darkness. Moonlight cast long shadows across the deck; perfect for clandestine rendezvous and nefarious acts. The paddle wheel chugged rhythmically, splashing water against the hull. The rigging slapped softly on the masts.

A gentle breeze tugged at Jack's jacket, as he escorted the

maid toward the wheel housing.

"What if the Parsons return early?" She scanned the darkened cabin windows along the deck.

Jack unhooked the safety rope from the rail and stepped aside. Steps led down, along the paddle wheel housing, to an observation platform.

She paused at the top of the steps. "Are we allowed down there?" she asked.

So close.

Jack dug his fingers into his palm. His heart thumped.

Patience.

"I must apologise. I never did ask your name," he said.

"Mary," she replied.

"I knew a Mary once."

"A girlfriend?"

"A gentleman doesn't tell."

She hesitated.

"I'm not that kind of girl," she said.

"I'm not that kind of gentleman," he replied.

Mary smiled.

Almost there. He puffed on his cigarillo and let the vapour envelop them.

"It could be the only adventure you get to have on the voyage." He tapped the case and offered her a cigarillo. "And I won't tell the Parsons."

She grinned, took the cigarillo and descended the stairs.

Jack removed his top hat and walking cane, secured them in a nearby lifeboat, and followed. The wind whipped along the edges of the platform. He could taste the salt as the sea spray settled on his shoulders.

"You can taste the sea!" Mary's words whipped away in the wind squall as she leaned out over the rail and sucked on her cigarillo. Its orange glow pinpointed her position in the dark.

Jack snatched the cigarillo from his own lips and flicked it across the deck. He slipped the glove off his mechanical hand, swapped it for a handkerchief from his pocket, and wrapped it around his fingers. He stepped forward, towards the flickering orange light of the cigarillo end, and slipped the makeshift garrotte around Mary's neck.

Her cigarillo plummeted into the water. She clawed at the material. A scream gurgled in her throat as she squirmed and twisted to face him.

Jack stared into her eyes: wide open, pupils flaring at him in accusation. His heart skipped. He grunted and tightened the handkerchief between his metal fingers.

Mary wriggled and gasped for air.

He nuzzled his cheek against her neck. The smell of lavender and tobacco tantalised his nostrils.

"Hush," he whispered. "You should be grateful. You'll help save thousands."

Her scream was silent. Her eyelids twitched. She stopped struggling. A convulsion rippled through her body.

Jack released the pressure on the handkerchief. Her head lulled forward. His heart raced. He cradled the body in his arms and listened. A faint warm breath tickled his skin. It was ragged, but it was there.

He lowered the body onto the deck, unrolled a leather pouch and removed a large-needled syringe. After years of experience, he worked swiftly in the shadows. When the collection was complete, and the blood samples secured, he eyed the pale corpse now pocked with exsanguination marks.

Jack covered his jacket with the maid's apron, and

squatted by the body. With a flick of his wrist, a seven inch blade slid from its sheath hidden in his mechanical arm. There must be no evidence left of his work. He sliced along her arms to conceal the puncture wounds. The skin was still warm. Blood flicked from his blade as he cut the torso.

Faint light flickered across the waves. He glanced back toward the deck. A few cabin lights winked at him.

He rose to his feet. Blood pooled and glistened on the platform; its sharp, metallic smell, mixed with salt caught on the wind. He wiped a wet fleck from his cheek and frowned. He'd been too enthusiastic.

He rolled the body over the rail, wiped his blade and snapped it back into its sheath, then removed the bloodied apron and tossed it into the wind. It fluttered, caught in the wheel and plunged into the sea where the body had fallen.

Jack watched the turning wheel and smiled. It would conceal his work nicely.

The cabin door rattled. A muffled voice came from the passage outside.

"Doctor Collins?"

Jack rolled over in his bed. His right hand snatched up the harness of his prosthetic arm. He shoved it onto the stump of his left forearm and snapped the clasps in place. Gears ticked inside the prosthetic. The metal finger joints whirred in response.

Another knock.

Jack glanced at the porthole. The curtains fluttered in the breeze. Light barely illuminated the material. He rummaged in his jacket pocket for his watch, and flipped it open; over an hour until breakfast.

He growled and grabbed his dressing robe off the hook by the bed.

"Evans, I left orders not to be disturbed."

He strode past his workbench, cranked the handle of the Centrifugal Cellular Separating Device.

A third knock. Louder this time.

"Sir?"

Jack dragged on his robe, strode into the suite's Sitting Room and yanked open the cabin door.

"Evans, you better have a damn g—"

The steward lowered his hand.

"Yes, Mr Cox?"

"I apologise for the early hour, Doctor Collins," replied the steward, "but the Captain needs to speak with you, urgently."

Jack sucked in a quick breath. They'd found the maid's body sooner than expected. He wrapped his robe around his naked torso, knotted the sash and jerked the robe's sleeve down over his un-gloved mechanical hand.

A breeze tickled the hairs on the back of his neck. His metal wrist twitched. The laboratory! He'd left the adjoining door open.

He resisted the urge to unsheathe the blade and rid himself of this nuisance. He moved to block Cox's view and stared directly into his eyes. Cox averted his gaze, settling it on the untouched, full champagne glass sitting on the table next to the settee- in the opposite direction of the laboratory door.

Jack's lip curled. They always looked away.

"May I inquire as to the nature of his business?" Jack clasped his hands behind his back.

"I'm sorry, sir. I was just ordered to bring you to the Captain." Cox hesitated, still unable to look Jack in the eye. "It is urgent, sir."

"I am permitted to dress." It was a statement, not a question; he wanted to watch the man squirm.

"Of course, sir." Cox's gaze remained fixed on the champagne glass. "I'll wait outside, sir."

Jack locked the cabin and followed Cox's eyeline to his private quarters. The door opened inward, blocking the view of his makeshift laboratory. He leaned on the wall and let out a slow breath. Fortune had favoured him, yet again. One day it would run out.

Cox ushered Jack to the Medical quarters at the rear of the First Class passengers' cabins. The large cabin was pristine and sparsely furnished. A metal-framed partition, with a gathered linen curtain, divided the room, obscuring the back of the cabin.

A middle-aged, dark-haired man, dressed in black with a beige apron and wire-rimmed spectacles perched on his forehead, bent over a small microscope. He stared into the eyepieces and frowned.

Cox tapped on the door frame.

"Excuse me, Doctor Bucknall. The police surgeon is here."

The physician straightened up, wiped his hands on his apron, then slipped his spectacles back onto his nose.

"Ah, Doctor Collins." He proffered his hand. "I'm Doctor Bucknall."

Jack eyed his un-gloved hand and nodded in greeting. "I was told the Captain had urgent business."

"Ah, yes. Apologies. It's all terribly unexpected," said Bucknall. "He will be here shortly." He picked up a syringe, tapped its barrel and rose from his chair.

Jack's fingers twitched. He'd left his blade behind in his cabin. He clenched his teeth.

"Follow me," said Bucknall.

Jack eyed the syringe. The physician led him towards the temporary partition, and pushed it to one side.

Two cot beds lined the cabin walls, a closed door between them. The bed on the left was occupied by an ashen-faced gentleman. Jack recognised him as Mr. Ivers, who had complained about the tube lighting. His starched collar had been removed; flecks of blood marred the neckband. His shirt was unbuttoned. One sleeve was rolled up to reveal his pale arm. A blood-spattered enamelled dish and rags sat on a trolley next to the bed.

"What's wrong with the gentleman?" asked Jack.

"He's quarantined," replied Bucknall, "with possible flu. Best not get too close." He swabbed the man's arm and jabbed the needle into the skin.

The patient moaned quietly, ignoring their presence.

"What are you giving him?" asked Jack.

"Mercury Cure and Colloid Silver," replied Bucknall.

"Mercury cure for the influenza?"

"Possible influenza. We don't know what ails him, and I have to be sure. We can't afford it to spread to the other passengers."

Bucknall removed the needle. Silvered droplets dripped onto the linen sheets.

Jack grimaced. "May I examine the patient?"

Bucknall nodded and retreated from the bed.

Jack examined the man. The skin around the injection site was bluish grey. Ivers' fingers trembled. Jack pinched the patient's skin. No reaction. He inspected his eyes. The pupils were dilated.

Jack clenched his mechanical fingers; he loathed incompetence. Already the tell-tale signs of overdose were there: numbness and tremors. He'd seen it before, when working in the Royal London Hospital. Whitechapel was rife with charlatans using the Mercury Cure for anything and everything. But Ivers hadn't shown any obvious signs of mercury poisoning at dinner last night; mercury poisoning required high doses or long exposure. How could Bucknall have missed them?

Jack inspected the labels of the medicine bottle on the trolley: Colloidal Silver, Mercury. Five times the usual dose. The quack; he was the sort that gave doctors a dubious reputation.

"Is this what you're giving him?" asked Jack. Bucknall nodded.

"How long have you been a ship's doctor?" asked Jack.

"Twenty-six years."

"Did you check he wasn't taking the Mercury Cure for anything else?"

Bucknall didn't answer.

Cox cleared his throat, and hovered near the partition.

"Excuse me, Doctors, but the Captain insisted you begin immediately."

"Yes, yes." Bucknall turned his back on his patient and unlocked the far door.

Jack raised an eyebrow.

Bucknall wrinkled his nose as he ushered Jack into the

unlit cabin.

Jack smelled it too; the unmistakable stench of recent death. He knew it well.

The light tube crackled. Its sickly blue light illuminated the cabin. A body, wrapped in a dark-stained linen sheet, lay packed with ice in a metal tub.

"Good morning, Captain." Cox retreated to the other side of the partition.

Jack's shoulders stiffened. It had all been a ruse; even a ship's doctor, dealing only with bellyaches and over-indulgence of alcohol could not possibly be so incompetent. The bastards knew how to play the game. He thrummed his gloved fingers on his palm. How did they suspect him so soon? He'd been careful. And he didn't make mistakes.

He clenched his fist. He was surrounded; too many to defeat without his blade. He surveyed the makeshift morgue. No windows. Only the one exit. No escape. Even if he could, he was trapped on a steamship, in the middle of the Atlantic. His heart raced. He longed for the anonymity of London's endless foggy warrens.

Jack took a deep, calming breath and turned to greet the Captain.

The Captain was a well-dressed gentleman, with greying hair. He carried his white cap under one arm, and extended his other hand in greeting.

"Welcome, Doctor Collins. Captain Cates, at your service. I do apologise for the ungodly hour, but I'd like to have this unfortunate incident sorted before luncheon, if possible."

"Unfortunate incident?" Jack mentally calculated his chances of dispatching all three men, and escaping unnoticed.

"We can't allow the passengers to learn of a suspicious death," replied the Captain. "It could cause panic." He nodded in the direction of the ship's doctor. "And Bucknall here is unsure if it is a suspicious death."

Bucknall unwrapped the linen cloth and folded it back to reveal the maid's face. Purple bruises blemished her pale skin.

"You've worked as a police surgeon," said Captain Cates. "I am officially requesting your assistance. I need to know if this poor lass took her own life, or if I have a murderer on my ship."

"We're fortunate to have someone more experienced in these matters." Bucknall lowered his voice. "This is beyond my expertise, I'm afraid."

Jack blinked. His fingers relaxed. His borrowed identity had an unexpected advantage. He listed the post mortem examination procedures he'd learned at University, in his head. It had been several years since he'd performed cutting procedures 'by the book.'

"May I assist?" asked Bucknall.

Jack gritted his teeth. He preferred to work alone, but there was no plausible reason he could give to exclude the ship's doctor. This time his work would have to look more... polite.

"I'll fetch my instruments," he said.

The body of Mary - last name still unknown - was unremarkable, except for the bruising around the temples, a longitudinal incision along the left wrist and forearm. Deep wounds cut throughout her torso, and a jagged laceration encircled her neck almost obscuring the strangulation bruises.

Doctor Bucknall hovered behind him, notebook in hand.

"Open the skylight," Jack said.

He slipped on an apron, rolled up his sleeves and leaned over the body to examine the hands. The nails were torn, fingers bruised. He checked under the nails. Any incriminating evidence had been washed away. Excellent.

Next he examined the head. The face was swollen. Clouded corneas stared back at him. Red flecks scarred the sclera.

Jack eyed his unwanted assistant. The man's face was pale, his attention fixated on the larger wounds in the abdomen. Jack smiled. He was certain Bucknall wouldn't notice the eyes, nor the swollen tongue.

"No indications of a struggle." He closed the eyelids and stepped back. "Bruising to the face and torso are consistent with damage from the paddle wheel."

Bucknall scribbled down the lie in his notebook.

Jack pulled back the collar of the bodice and pressed the epidermis. He'd have preferred the body to remain in the water longer...

Bucknall stared blankly at the corpse; the man seemed oblivious to Jack's findings and willing to accept anything reported.

Jack was in control. Still, he couldn't be too careful; people forgot themselves at sea. Bucknall was proof of that. He took a deep breath and focused. He would not succumb to the lure of the sea.

"Where was the body found?" he asked.

Bucknall snapped his attention away from the corpse. "In the water, near the paddle wheel housing."

"That's consistent with the skin texture." Jack prodded

the epidermis. "See? I'd say the body had been in the water only a few hours."

Bucknall's cheeks bulged. He stepped back, and jotted in his notebook.

"How long has it been since you examined a body?" asked Jack.

"September, 1880," replied Bucknall. "Heart attack. Died in his sleep."

Jack relaxed. There was little chance Bucknall would scrutinise his procedure.

"Let's get a closer look at those injuries, shall we?"

Bucknall turned his head.

Jack smirked. He unbuttoned the bodice and peeled away the fabric. Several deep wounds slashed the abdomen and torso. He closed his eyes. His muscle memory marked each one: a few inches from the left was a jagged tear, cutting through the tissue. Four more cuts downward. He opened his eyes.

"Paddle wheel, you say?"

Bucknall nodded his head. "Yes."

"That would be consistent with these injuries." Another lie. "I think, the lungs first."

He cracked open the ribcage and pushed the knife into the thorax.

Bucknall winced. "I'll get the trolley." He scurried from the room.

The grey lungs squelched as they were removed. Jack squeezed. Black liquid dribbled from the tissue. There was no pulmonary oedema.

Bucknall wheeled a trolley into the room.

Jack plopped the lung into one of the enamelled dishes on it. He shook his head.

"No water in the lung?" asked Bucknall.

Jack froze. Perhaps the man wasn't as incompetent he seemed.

"She must have died before she entered the water," he said.

"Suicide then?" Bucknall eyed the long incisions along the left wrist, avoiding the dissected torso open between them.

"It appears so." An untruth was more believable if backed up with facts. "The poor girl was obviously distressed and took her own life. She bled out before she entered the water, and was dragged under the wheel."

"But there would have been more blood on the observation platform." Bucknall frowned.

"The water washed it away."

The creases in Bucknall's forehead faded. He nodded slowly.

Jack removed the remaining organs, placed them in dishes on the trolley and examined each one in turn, keeping up the pretence.

Bucknall scribbled more notes.

Metal squeaked in the other room. A quick movement caught the corner of Jack's eye. His head jerked in its direction.

"What was that?"

"I didn't hear—"

"I thought you locked the door." Jack's knife clattered onto the metal trolley.

He pushed past Bucknall, and elbowed aside the temporary partition. The cabin door was open.

There was a faint rustle. A flash of red. He dashed to the doorway and peered along the passageway. It was empty.

Jack thumped the door frame with his mechanical hand; metal cogs whirred in protest. His instincts rarely betrayed him.

He clicked the door shut and surveyed the cabin. The medicines were locked away. The instruments seemed to be in order. Nothing had been meddled with.

The gentleman patient moaned. His collar had been pulled askew. Blood trickled down his neck from an unhealed puncture mark of a large gauge needle.

Jack frowned. He pulled the collar back further to examine the wound more closely. There was not one, but two puncture marks. Jack sucked in a sharp breath. Catherine used to devour Penny Dreadful novels, with their stories of creatures that fed on blood. He shook his head.

Vampyres didn't exist.

Rivals

Waiters paced after the mechanical food and drink trolleys as they progressed through the Dining Room. The lights buzzed fitfully. They'd been malfunctioning all day, as if mourning the maid's death.

Piano music wafted across the tables, riding the warm Mediterranean breeze trickling through the open windows. Steam rose from the music machine, drifted into the draught and dissipated over the closest tables.

Jack sat in his corner, sipped his water and skimmed the menu: hare soup, fried fillet of fish, Poulet a la Marento, followed by a generous list of roasts and vegetables. He peered over the menu card and eyed the familiar diners, who occupied their designated seats.

Mrs. Ivers sat at her nearby table, picking at her food. She'd dined alone since her husband had been isolated in quarantine. Still, she kept up appearances, with not a hair out of place; obviously the steward had found her alternative lighting. The waiters delivered notes of condolence from gawping diners unwilling to approach her for fear of contagion.

Lord Sebastian and his mother had been relocated to a table on the other side of Jack, away from potential contamination. Every night, the young Lord fawned over his mother, while eyeing the young ladies - married or not - over the rim of his continually-refilled wine glass.

With a loud pop, the tube lights by the entrance fizzled out. Darkness cascaded across the room.

The whir of the trolleys ceased. A metal utensil clattered on a china plate.

"Must I dine in the dark?" Mrs. Ivers' voice broke the silence.

There was a scuffle, not too far away.

Jack's blade sang quietly as it slipped into his palm.

"Will they never fix those things!" Mrs. Ivers growled. "This is what happens when one relies on these new-fangled gadgets. The Queen would never stand for it."

Waiters appeared in the entrance, and ferried lit candelabra to the tables. The warm candlelight cast a shadow across Jack's menu.

The sweet fragrance of rose caressed his nostrils. Black, silk-gloved fingers curled over the top of the menu card, and slipped it from his hand.

"I took the liberty of ordering for us both." The voice was silky, the words almost sung, rather than spoken.

Jack glanced up. Lady Ambrose, an elegant woman with an alluring smile and piercing green eyes, swept up her crimson skirts and leaned forward, presenting her décolletage as she slid into the chair beside him.

A food trolley trundled up to their table. The Head Waiter laid their plates before them: roast beef - rare and moist -

and baked potatoes. He presented the Lady Ambrose with a bottle of red wine. She nodded. He filled her glass and turned to face Jack.

Jack shook his head and slipped his hand over his wine glass.

"Would you prefer tea, sir?" asked the Head Waiter.

Jack nodded.

Lady Ambrose raised an eyebrow.

The Head Waiter waved over the drinks trolley, poured a fresh cup of tea and excused himself.

Lady Ambrose tugged the buttons at the wrists of her silk gloves and peeled them off her hands. A wave of perfume embraced Jack.

"How very British," she said. "You don't drink wine?"

"Alcohol dulls the mind." He pressed his blade back into its sheath.

"Only if one over-indulges." Dark auburn curls cascaded over her alabaster shoulders.

She smiled. A perfect smile. Perfect lips. Perfect eyes. Jack's heart skipped. She reminded him of...

"Have we met before?" He stirred his tea, careful not to touch the sides of his cup.

"You're very forward, sir." Her voice; if he closed his eyes, he could imagine...

He took a deep breath. Catherine was dead. By his own hand. Dead and buried. For science.

"Forgive me." He couldn't tear his gaze away from those eyes. He forced a blink. "You remind me of someone."

"A lover?" She sipped her wine slowly and gazed at him. No, past him.

He followed her gaze to the, admittedly handsome, young Lord dining with his mother.

"It was a long time ago." Jack dissected his roast beef, scraping his fork on the china plate.

Lady Ambrose's attention snapped back to Jack.

"That's a shame." She took a deep breath. "A man in his prime." She sipped the wine; her tongue licked an errant drop from her lips.

"Me, or Lord Sebastian?" he asked.

"A man may enjoy a tasty morsel, may he not?" Lady Ambrose replied. "But if a Lady is peckish, she is condemned." She grinned. "I prefer a full meal, accompanied by a more mature wine."

A smile twitched over Jack's lips. Her tongue was quick. Just like dear Catherine.

Her green eyes flashed in the candlelight. Intriguing. Intelligent.

He drew a slow breath. It'd been a long time since he'd enjoyed female company. He shifted in his chair and stretched his fingers. Perhaps he should enjoy the delights of the voyage? Once he arrived in the Colonies, work would consume him.

Lady Ambrose poked at her roast beef with her fork. Its juice had seeped into the potato.

"Is the beef not to your liking?" he asked.

She pushed the vegetables to one side.

"If you are unwell, I may be able to assist." He laid his cutlery on his plate. "I am a doctor."

"I thought you had that smell about you." She leaned forward. Her breast rose and fell quickly. "Didn't you attend to the girl, who—" She paused.

Jack's mechanical hand twitched under the table. The other passengers seemed oblivious to the maid's fate. The captain seemed content with Jack's reported findings. He'd thought he was safe.

She lowered her voice to a whisper: "Such a tragedy."

He nodded.

His trouser hem fluttered. Something touched his ankle and slowly brushed along his calf.

"It's been a long time since I had..." her eyelids fluttered, "a thorough examination."

Jack's pulse quickened.

He slipped his right hand across the table towards her.

Lady Ambrose leaned forward; she smelled of roses and honey. She placed her hand on his. Her hand was cold.

"Perhaps we could...?" She sighed, obviously well-versed in displaying her attributes to their best advantage. "Perhaps you could escort me back to my cabin? It's not far, and the lighting has malfunctioned."

Jack glanced around the dining room. Lord Sebastian grinned and nodded in his direction. It would be unseemly to be seen visiting her cabin. Society, even on holiday, could be ruthless. And he, despite his sins, was still a gentleman.

"Perhaps my cabin?" he whispered.

"Yes." She squeezed his hand.

"In that case, I am honoured, Lady Ambrose." He rose from his chair and offered her his arm.

"Please, call me Charlotte," she whispered as she slipped her arm around his. "Thank you, Doctor Collins."

"My friends call me Jack."

The light tube in Jack's cabin crackled and dimmed. It appeared the entire ship was in danger of technological failure. Jack lit the lamp on the side table.

Charlotte surveyed the sitting room, her gaze pausing on the unopened bottle of champagne and clean champagne flutes on the table by the settee.

"I thought you didn't drink, Jack?" The corner of her lip curled.

He returned the smile.

"I believe I said it dulls the brain," he replied.

Charlotte opened the bottle, filled two glasses and offered one to Jack.

She circled the room, glass in hand, and halted near the open door leading to the bedroom.

Jack's mechanical hand twitched. The blade clicked in its sheath. His polite smile dropped. He hadn't intended on inviting anyone into his sanctuary. He silently cursed. He'd left an experiment running whilst he had dinner.

He stepped in front of the door, blocking her view.

"I hadn't expected company," he said.

She clicked her tongue. "I assure you, I am not easily shocked."

Jack slipped his hand around her waist, intending to sweep her away from his makeshift laboratory.

She kissed him on the cheek and unpinned her curls. Her hair caressed his neck, enveloping him in the aroma of honey and fine wine. He closed his eyes and breathed in the intoxicating perfume.

Charlotte clasped his hand with strong fingers, spun out of his embrace and glided through the doorway. Jack growled under his breath, yanked the glove off his mechanical hand and strode after her. He could not afford to have his work exposed or his samples corrupted.

Instead of a scream, Charlotte smiled. Jack hesitated, the

blade tip resting on his fingertip, ready to strike.

"I thought you were a police surgeon?" she said.

"How did you—?" Jack frowned. "I never mentioned my occupation."

"The steward knows everything." She giggled. "I don't seduce just anyone, my dear Jack."

"I thought I was seducing you." Jack closed the door behind him; it would help muffle the scream.

She laughed; this time it was no girlish giggle.

"That is what women like men to believe." She placed her champagne glass on the workbench. "It's less complicated that way." She slipped off her long gloves, rolled them up and placed them next to her glass.

"Are you an experimental chemist?" She circled the workbench, halted on the opposite side, and examined the array of glass vials suspended from metal rods. Above it was a pear-shaped glass funnel, its dripper still containing remnants of a red liquid. She sniffed the vial below it, containing dark clumps, suspended in yellow liquid.

Jack hesitated.

She stiffened; her eyes widened.

No scream? Jack's heart raced.

"I specialise in haematology," he said. "That's the study of—"

"Blood." Her pupils flared.

"How did you know?"

"My dear, departed husband was a scientist. As was I." She turned to examine the row of research books on the table under the window and ran her finger along the spine of a book. "I have a fascination for men of science."

She glanced at his mechanical hand and smiled.

"I see your work pays well." She returned her attention to

the blood-filled vial.

"Is this why you're travelling halfway around the world?" she asked.

Jack nodded. "Australia is more liberal in its attitude to research."

"And the Queen has less control?" she whispered.

"It is advantag—"

He felt the touch of her soft, cool skin on his hand. His fingers twitched. How had she moved so fast? His brain buzzed. He shook his head.

She extracted the full champagne glass from his hand and placed it on the table next to the bed.

"May I ask, what takes you to the southern regions of Australia?" Jack let his muscles relax.

"I've been sent to expand the family business." She slipped her fingers between his and stroked his mechanical hand. "Tell me, is it painful?"

Jack opened his mouth to reply.

"Shhh." She pressed her finger against his lips. "It has been a long time since my husband died."

As she kissed him, she slid her hand under his dinner jacket and rested her hand on his chest, over his heart.

Jack closed his eyes, and savoured pleasant memories, pushing away visions of Catherine lying in her own blood. Whitechapel was across the ocean, in the past. He'd paid a high price. He deserved a little compensation.

"What's wrong?" she asked.

"Oh, just memories."

"Of what?" she asked.

"One doesn't compare lovers."

"Why not?" She giggled. Her cold lips kissed his neck. She slipped off his dinner jacket and tossed it on the floor.

She sniffed his neck.

"You smell of—" She hissed and pushed him away.

Pain seared up his right arm. Jack's eyes snapped open. He wrenched his metal hand free from her grip. He flicked the blade free and thrust it into her chest.

She stared into his eyes. The corner of Jack's lip curled as his gaze locked onto hers. No one could withstand what they found there. Her eyes widened. There was fear.

Sharp eyeteeth protruded onto her lower lip. Her black eyes burned. Jack's heart skipped.

She stepped back and eased the blade from her torso. Her bodice was ripped, but there was little blood.

"What are you?" he whispered.

"Some call us *strigoi*. Others: Vampyre. To you, I am death."

Jack's mind raced. Vampyre? Impossible! They didn't exist.

He shook his head. It wouldn't be long before she remembered he was only human. He had to prove he was worth more alive; everyone had their price. What could he offer her? What had Catherine's books said? 'Vampyres feed on fresh blood.' But, his blood samples were stale.

Fresh blood? His smile returned. As a doctor, he had access to the quarantine quarters.

She circled towards the door, holding his blade in her hand. Her gaze shifted downward on his neck. Her eyelids fluttered.

"I should rip your throat out," she growled.

"And what after that?" His voice remained calm. "How would you explain my death?"

She scoffed. "The Captain will do anything I tell him. He's as weak as the ship's doctor."

Her eyes narrowed.

Jack felt her inside his head, rummaging around, rattling locks, looking for a way in. He had to concentrate.

The metal joints of his hand clicked as he raised it between them.

Get out of my head!

She winced. "How—?"

Jack's heartbeat slowed. She couldn't control him, and that scared her.

"I understand what you are, and I'm not afraid," he whispered. "We can help each other. You control Bucknall; he won't question my authority. I can quarantine as many patients as you need. I, in turn, get all the samples I need to continue my work until we reach Australia."

She edged closer. There was still fire in her eyes.

"You're a scientist - or were one. Surely, you can understand the logic of it." Jack held his ground. He understood the struggle of intellect over desire. "But I need to know I can trust you."

She paused. The fire in her eyes cooled. Jack lowered his hand.

"I am not a savage. I can control myself!" She grinned. Her eyeteeth dented her lips. "Most of the time." Her eyes glinted green in the lamplight.

Jack took a deep breath. "Then we have a deal?"

She nodded and dropped onto the edge of the bed.

"I must feed."

Jack didn't move. It could be a ruse to catch him off guard.

"I promise I won't attack you." Her eyelids drooped. The fire in her eyes was gone. She offered him the hilt of his knife. She bared her teeth; the extended eyeteeth had retracted.

Jack inched forward and took the knife.

"You know my weakness," whispered Charlotte. "Can I trust you to keep to your bargain?"

Jack placed the knife on the table by the bed, next to his champagne glass. He extended his right hand towards her and helped her to her feet.

"Dear Humphry understood me too, Jack." She leaned her head on his shoulder.

"I prescribe a visit to the medical quarters."

"But Mr. Ivers' blood is tainted." Her shoulders slumped.

"I believe his wife visits her husband every evening, after dinner."

She managed a faint smile, as if to show him that her teeth were still retracted, then closed her mouth and kissed his wrist. "Oh, we shall have such sport together, young Jack."

He patted her hand; the skin was ice cold.

"Eat first, then play," he whispered.

Truce

ack had dreamed of Catherine, risen from the grave, beautiful and willing. He stretched his arms and opened his eyes. Sunlight glared across the rumpled sheets on the floor and streamed across his face. He raised his right hand to shield his face from the light and flipped over onto the opposite side of the bed, out of the direct sunlight, and pushed himself up onto his elbows and surveyed the room.

Charlotte was gone. He was alone.

On the bedside table, next to Jack's still-full champagne flute was a perfectly calligraphed note:

I keep my promises. I look forward to dinner tonight. Eat, then play.
Lottie.

Jack slid to the side of the bed and examined himself in a hand mirror. There were two small bruises on his shoulder; the skin was unbroken. He examined the rest of his skin.

There were no puncture marks. She'd kept her word.

He dropped the mirror on the bed and laughed. He had a new playmate, who understood all his desires, and supported his experiments. Something Catherine could never have done.

He pulled on a clean pair of trousers, attached his prosthetic arm and reached for his blood-stained knife. A rivulet of thick blood rolled along the groove of the blade. It had not yet coagulated.

Jack checked his pocket watch: eight hours. He raised an eyebrow.

He balanced the blade, so as not to lose the precious sample, and drained it into a clean vial, then transferred drops onto a glass slide. Flakes of dried blood from his previous sample were added to the slide. He placed it under the microscope.

Charlotte's blood engulfed the dried flecks and mixed with the red blood cells. He waited. The mixed sample didn't re-coagulate.

Jack leaned back in his chair and let out a long, slow breath.

"Bloody hell." Was this the answer? Had he found a way to create an all-purpose donor for blood transfusions?

His heart raced. Perhaps he could ask Lottie for more samples? Or would that destroy their pact? He eyed the vial of her blood. He had enough for now. It could wait. There was almost two months before the voyage ended. Two months of pleasure. Two months before he had to make a final decision.

Jack wiped his blade and snapped it into its sheath. He slipped on a fresh linen shirt, apologising silently to Catherine as he folded Charlotte's note and slid it into the pocket, next to his heart.

He tied his cravat high on his neck and rolled up his shirt sleeves. He had some experimenting to do before dinner.

Jack surveyed the commandeered crew quarters, lined with over a dozen occupied bunk beds, adequate 'quarantine' quarters for those deemed to be suffering from influenza.

Once the word of a possible outbreak had spread, the Captain had demanded affected passengers be isolated, and put Jack in charge of quarantine. He had avoided the crew quarters since. The threat of infection kept nosy visitors away.

The past eight weeks had been both exhilarating and exhausting. Quarantine had provided a convenient source for experimental samples. He'd already isolated three different blood types, confirming his initial theory.

Jack slid the needle into Mrs. Ivers' arm. Her skin was thin and pale and dehydrated. She twitched on the crew's bunk bed. Her eyes stared past him, fixating on whatever alternate reality Charlotte had concocted. He drew back the plunger. Blood filled the barrel.

"Sleep, Mrs. Ivers," he whispered. "It's just a dream."

Mrs. Ivers closed her eyes.

Jack transferred the blood sample into a glass tube and stoppered it. It clinked as it joined the other vials in his bag.

Lady Charlotte Ambrose drifted into the cabin and clicked the door shut behind her. She was a vision in scarlet silk and lace.

Jack's heart raced.

"I felt a little peckish." She unpinned her bonnet, placed

it on the table in front of him and drifted along the row of beds.

Jack closed his bag and followed her.

"I feel like..." Charlotte hovered near Mrs. Ivers' body and sniffed. Her eyes widened, her pupils dilated. "Was she part of today's collection?"

Jack nodded.

Charlotte leaned closer. Mrs. Ivers stirred and opened her eyes.

"She has such sweet blood for one with such a sharp tongue, unlike her husband." She glanced at Jack and smiled. Her smile twisted as her eyeteeth elongated. "Excellent choice, my love."

"Time to dance." She ran her fingers through Mrs. Ivers' blonde locks.

Mrs. Ivers rose slowly, held out her hand and smiled. Charlotte took it, reeled her in and wrapped her arm around Mrs. Ivers' uncorseted body. They swayed for a moment; a bizarre ritual, but one Jack had come to enjoy, almost as much as he did Lottie.

They floated, skirts entwined. Charlotte twirled her 'partner' between them. Their silk skirts rustled and brushed against Jack's hand.

Charlotte stared into his eyes, as if trying to reach the darkness in his soul.

His head thumped. Everyone craved something; some lusted after power, some chemical addictions, others: love. Blood tied them together; a bond stronger than mere love. It was their mutual addiction. They both craved it. She to survive, he to help others survive.

A smile flickered over Charlotte's lips. Her teeth pressed against Mrs. Ivers' wrist and pushed slowly through the skin.

Jack dug his fingers into his palms, as she pierced the flesh. He could hear the blood rushing into her mouth.

Mrs. Ivers moaned. Blood seeped from the wound. Charlotte's tongue flicked across Mrs. Ivers' wrist. Charlotte's eyes rolled back. She latched onto the wrist and sucked with more vigour.

Jack envied her control. One day he would master such self-control. He would not reprise the mistake he made with the maid.

The cabin door rattled. A knock followed.

"Doctor Collins?"

"It's the blasted doctor," hissed Jack.

Charlotte glanced up briefly, her eyes unfocused, then returned to her feast.

Jack rolled down his shirt sleeves and approached the door.

"What do you want, Doctor Bucknall?" he asked.

"We're two days from port. The Captain wants an update. The Port Adelaide authorities won't allow us to dock with an influenza epidemic on board."

Jack turned to face Charlotte. He knew better than to interrupt her.

She growled, unlatched herself, and released her grip. Mrs. Ivers slumped onto her bunk.

"Let the beastly man in."

Jack swallowed. "Are you sure?" he whispered.

She licked an errant drop of blood from her lips and nodded.

He turned the key in the lock and opened the door.

"Locking the door now, Doctor Collins?" Bucknall blustered into the cabin. "Any news on a cure yet?"

He strode past Charlotte, towards a single bed near Jack's

desk.

"How is Lady Sebastian? Any improvement? Her son has been asking after her."

Charlotte's eyelashes fluttered at the name. Something stirred in Jack's gut. Something new. He gritted his teeth. Was this what jealousy felt like?

"Perhaps he should visit her occasionally?" said Lottie. "I could do with some dessert."

"Shhh, he'll hear you," whispered Jack.

She laughed, entwined her fingers in his and draped herself over Jack's shoulder. A heady aroma of rose engulfed him.

"What was that, Doctor Collins?" Bucknall looked at Jack, and seemed to ignore Charlotte.

"Nothing," replied Jack.

"His mind is weak." Lottie extricated her fingers and moved closer to Bucknall. "He can't hear or see me until I tell him he can." Charlotte twirled in front of him. She would be the death of him.

"Are you feeling all right, Doctor Collins? You haven't succumbed to the flu, have you?" asked Bucknall.

Jack shook his head. "Two days until port?" he asked. Charlotte shadowed Bucknall as he returned to face Jack.

"Plenty of time to finish up here." She leaned past Bucknall and kissed Jack on the ear.

His heart pounded. He swallowed, trying not to react.

"Tell the Captain the experimental inoculation has been successful," he continued. "The patients are recovering. We should be able to dock safely."

"He'll be pleased to hear of your progress." Bucknall placed his doctor's bag on the desk. "One body is enough to declare to the authorities."

"Pardon?" Jack jerked his attention back to the ship's doctor.

"The suicide."

"I thought the body was buried at sea?"

"No, she's packed away in the ice house. The Captain didn't want anyone to get wind of it and upset the First Class passengers."

Jack swallowed. A real police surgeon would reveal his lie; a trained eye would spot the wounds were not self-inflicted, nor the results of a paddle wheel.

His gaze darted in Charlotte's direction, hovering behind Bucknall.

"What's wrong?" She frowned.

"I can't allow the body to be re-examined," he replied, ignoring Bucknall's presence. "She didn't commit suicide."

Bucknall glared at him. "What are you talking about, man?"

"Sloppy, Jack," she hissed. "If they investigate one body, they'll want to inspect them all."

She snatched up Bucknall's arm and pinned him against the end of the nearest bunk bed post, and sank her fangs into his neck. The bed thudded against the wall as she drank. He struggled.

Charlotte pushed harder on his forearms, until his hands paled. His fingers twitched.

"Lottie?" Jack gently placed his hand on her arm.

She growled - a deep, guttural sound, like a rabid dog not willing to share its spoils - and glared at him. Her eyes burned red, piercing through his. Her face contorted in both ecstasy and animal hunger.

Jack caught his breath. The stench of sickly sweet roses clawed at his eyes, invaded his nostrils and rifled through his memories. He sneered. It was the smell of betrayal.

He retreated.

She thrust her fangs deeper into Bucknall's neck. The bed scraped. She flicked her head. Skin ripped. She closed her eyes and rutted his neck, pushing deeper until blood burst from the jagged wound. Her tongue lashed out, sucking loudly as it gathered the escaping blood.

Bucknall's body convulsed. Charlotte moaned, and embraced the movement.

Jack flinched. In two days they would be free to leave the ship, free to start new lives, without fear of retribution for their sins. But how long until she lost control with him? He needed to strike before she turned on him.

He fingered the tip of his blade. Steel would not save him. He searched his memory for the tales Catherine had whispered to him in the dark. A stake through the heart? Silver? He backed into the table. His hand groped for Bucknall's bag for the silver nitrate.

Lady Ambrose sighed and extracted herself from the doctor's pale body. It crumpled onto the floor and stared at Jack with sunken eyes.

She wiped the corner of her mouth.

"Who'd have thought the fool would taste so delicious?" She skipped to Jack and kissed him on the mouth. A long, lingering kiss. Her auburn curls choked him with the smell of stale roses.

"New perfume?" he asked.

"Yes, do you like it?"

"It reminds me of..."

"Another past love?" She giggled. "We are made for each other, Jack."

She stared at him, with desire in her eyes. You're next,

they whispered. His muscles stiffened. He peeled her arms off him and moved to examine Bucknall's lifeless body. Deep gashes tore across the throat.

"What's wrong, Jack?"

"How can I explain another death?"

"The stupid man died of influenza. You can't work your miracles on everyone." She twirled and laughed. "He was careless; too many years tending to bruised egos. They'll need to burn the body, of course." She was by his ear now, whispering. The stench of betrayal followed her. "Which fortunately will destroy any signs to the contrary."

"Will he become... like you?" he asked.

"Heavens, no! I wouldn't want to be stuck with him for all eternity." She perched on the edge of the table. "It's all about the blood, isn't it?" She eyed Jack. "You only become one of us if you drink my blood."

Blood. The fresh blood samples... And her blood; uncongealed blood. It was as if lightning cracked through his brain. He glanced at the microscope. The blood riddle. If only he could...

Jack slid onto his chair.

He removed the slide from the microscope and placed it with his other samples. If he was to continue his experiment he would need more of her blood. He couldn't destroy her. He'd already sacrificed one love to science. Perhaps there was another way?

"An enquiring mind, even in adversity." She leaned over the table. "Did I tell you my first husband was a scientist?" She giggled. "I do love a man of intelligence. Always thinking, always planning."

Jack froze. Did she know?

She kissed him on the head.

"A beautiful brain." She leaned back over the table and stared into his eyes, her pupils now mere specks of black. "You're fascinating, Jack. I can never tell what you're thinking." She pushed his chair away from the table, lifted her skirts and plopped herself on his lap. "What are you thinking, Jack?"

He relaxed.

"Curiosity is good for the mind," he whispered.

She wobbled. Her head fell onto his chest.

"I thought feeding made you stronger?" he asked.

"Always the scientist." She closed her eyes and nuzzled his chest. "Eat, then play," she cooed.

"Later." An idea was forming in his mind.

She rose to her feet, shoved him away and stumbled back to an empty bed. Jack caught his breath; she was still too strong.

Jack rummaged through Bucknall's bag. The bottle of silver nitrate was nearly empty; Bucknall had wasted it on Mr. Ivers. He examined all the bottles, including a used bottle of Laudanum. The fool had been self-medicating.

Jack checked his pocket watch. The dinner gong would sound soon. He needed more time to think.

"You should change for dinner," he said.

"I love to watch you eat." Her speech was slurred. "And besides, Lord Sebastian might be there."

"Window shopping?" There was that stirring in his gut again. He ignored it. "For a little dessert?"

Her eyes widened.

"I knew you understood me." She clicked her tongue. "Better not. Too much of a good thing. I need to keep my head clear for the rest of the voyage."

She closed her eyes and fell onto the bed, arms

outstretched as if intoxicated. Now was his opportunity to kill her before she killed him. He hesitated. Keeping her 'alive' would ensure a continuous supply of base blood samples to continue his work.

She lay on the bed, waiting for him as she'd done many times before. Wanting. Trusting. Apparently harmless. He remembered their first night: his untouched champagne by the bed, and hers on the workbench.

Jack grinned. Alcohol? Could it be that easy? But, she drank wine every night at dinner. His smile slipped. Not alcohol. Bottles rattled as he moved Bucknall's bag. The Laudanum? Perhaps it worked on vampyre physiology just as it did on humans? If he concentrated it? Added in something more? He needed just enough to keep her under control until they left the steamship.

He lifted Bucknall's body off the floor; at least there wasn't too much blood. He'd get Evans to remove it to the ice house. He'd inform the Captain of the doctor's unfortunate demise, at dinner.

Jack smiled. His plan was almost complete.

The gong sounded along the hall. And with it, the final piece of Jack's plan clattered into place.

Endgame

It took only one day. An 'accidental' meeting in the Smoking Room. A bit of charm and truckle was all that was needed to befriend the handsome Lord Sebastian, the object of Lady Ambrose's wandering eye. That, and an expensive bottle of hundred-year old port, two Russian cigars and the promise of a personal, and private, introduction to Lady Charlotte Ambrose, one of the richest women on the ship.

The suggestion that his mother planned to disinherit him due to his promiscuous behaviour, prodded him even further towards this fate.

Alcohol and Laudanum-laced Absinthe had loosened the young Lord's tongue. He boasted he'd enjoyed every willing female on the ship. He seemed more intent on amusing himself than ensuring his mother's well-being. He was bored playing the dutiful son and heir.

Jack ushered Lord Sebastian along the passage, ducking the Lord's gesticulating hand as he swatted green pixies.

Jack grinned. Lady Ambrose would cringe in horror when she finally met the buffoon. He doubted even Sebastian's handsome face and enthusiasm could compensate for lack of intelligence.

But Jack knew all too well lust's hold could override rational decisions. Twice now, he'd felt its pull. The first had not ended well. He would not let it happen again.

He nudged the clueless Lord towards his cabin door and opened it.

The late afternoon sun streamed across the sitting room. He still had time to set his trap. He led Sebastian through the sitting room to the bedroom, leaned his walking stick against the chair, and removed Sebastian's jacket.

Sebastian unbuttoned his shirt and collapsed on the bed.

"Ah, champagne!" The bottle scraped along the bedside table.

Jack frowned. How much could the man drink and still function? Jack grabbed the bottle.

"You can celebrate later," he said. The fool deserved his fate.

The main cabin door clicked. The tube light fizzled out in the sitting room.

Jack removed his dinner gloves.

"Jack?" Charlotte's sweet voice rolled over his skin and grated like crystallised honey.

He dug his nails into his palm; he must remain in control.

"Wait here, Hubert," he said. "Remember how rich she is."

Sebastian relinquished the bottle, fell back onto the bed and grinned.

The trap was set.

Jack closed the curtains and stepped back into the sitting

room. Charlotte wrapped her arms around him and kissed him on the neck. Her hair tickled his nose. He held his breath and nibbled her ear; their traditional greeting.

"I've got a gift for you," he whispered.

"A gift?" She tugged at his shirt buttons.

"Not here. In the bedroom."

"I love surprises." She grinned and dragged him around the shadowed edges of the cabin and into the bedroom.

Lord Sebastian had already removed his shirt.

She gasped. "How can I resist such a tasty morsel?"

Jack's gut squirmed.

She kissed Jack hard, and licked his lips.

His heart raced. He'd made the correct decision. It was a matter of self-preservation.

He closed his eyes and kissed her back.

"We're perfect for each other," she whispered in his ear.

Jack let her hand slip from his. He'd miss her. He retreated to the padded armchair near his workbench.

She leaped on the bed and ran her hands over Sebastian's now-naked chest. He undid her bodice.

Jack resisted the urge to drag her off the bed.

"It's unseemly to play with one's food, in company." She waggled her finger and flung her leg over Sebastian's torso.

The fool grinned inanely. He was either still mesmerised by green fairies, or her persuasive mental charms had already taken hold.

She sniffed his neck. "He smells divine."

Her eyes blazed. Her fangs protruded below her lips. She grinned and launched herself at Sebastian's neck. He moaned. This time there were no dainty sips; squelching, sucking noises filled Jack's ears. The trap was sprung.

He puffed on his cigarillo, and waited for her to sate

herself.

Blood gurgled in her throat. She growled and lunged again.

Jack tried to ignore their gyrating bodies. An arm snaked out of the fray.

Jack flicked his wrist. The blade rang as it left its sheath. Nothing would ruin his plan. Sebastian would not leave the room alive. She must drink every drop.

Her clawed hand lashed out and caught Sebastian's pale wrist and wrenched it back onto the bed.

Every muscle in Jack's body tensed. He'd calculated the amount of Laudanum to add to the Absinthe, based on her recovery time after she'd gorged on Bucknall - and doubled it. It hadn't mattered if it was a lethal dose; the man would be dead before morning anyway. Jack shifted in his chair. He prayed it would be enough to sedate her.

Sebastian's feet twitched. He whimpered; a pleasant sound.

Jack inhaled a deep breath of tobacco smoke to steady his nerves, averted his eyes and thought of his ultimate prize: the vampyre's transmuted blood would unlock the answer to successful blood transfusion.

She pushed harder, her head swaying with her victim's movements. The body convulsed. The champagne bottle rattled on the table and smashed onto the floor. She snarled, flung back her head and rocked back onto her haunches. Her eyes blazed red in the darkened room.

Jack swallowed. Perhaps he'd miscalculated. He grasped his walking cane: ash wood tipped with a silver spike. White oak would have been better. It wouldn't kill her, but it could slow her down.

"Jack?" Her voice was no longer melodic, but the rasp of

a hoarse daemon. "I need you, Jack." She sniffed the air and stretched a shapely leg out towards the floor.

Blood dribbled from the corner of her mouth, trickled down her neck, and between her breasts.

"Join me," she whispered. "Be with me forever." She slit her wrist with a sharp talon.

Jack's stomach clenched. Bile filled his mouth.

She wobbled.

He held his breath.

She fell forward onto her elbows, and giggled.

Jack let his breath escape slowly.

She rolled onto the bed, next to the drained corpse and wiggled her fingers at the ceiling.

"Hello," she cooed at the air. "Want to join me for dinner?"

Jack took a last puff of restorative smoke and crushed his cigarillo into a Petrie dish. He rose slowly. Glass crunched under his boots as he approached the bed.

"Shh," she murmured. "Someone's come to play."

Jack clutched his silver-headed cane and circled the bed.

"I think I broke your present." She reached out towards him and ran her fingers up his inside leg; the talons were gone, as were her fangs. "Have you come to rescue me, Jack?"

Jack extracted her fingers. Her hand fell into her lap. Her eyelids fluttered.

"Time to rest," he said. "We dock tomorrow, at noon. There are forms to sign before we arrive."

He retrieved papers from his workbench, pressed an ink-filled pen into her hand and indicated where to sign. She scribbled on the paper.

"Did we have fun?" She smiled.

"Oh, yes." He folded up the papers and tucked them in his pocket.

"Good." She buried her head into the blood-spattered pillow.

Jack checked her pulse, out of habit. Non-existent. That proved nothing; he had no idea if her sort had one. He slipped his fingers between hers and squeezed. Nothing. He peeled open an eyelid. Green eyes stared back at him, the pinpoint pupils fixed. She didn't stir.

Jack moved quickly. He didn't know how long he had. He tapped his cane on the wall closest to the passageway.

A key rattled in the door lock. Evans entered, pushing a medical gurney with a large sack on it. He locked the door behind him.

"Is it done, sir?" he asked.

"For now," replied Jack. "But we must hurry."

Together they swaddled the comatose Lady Ambrose in a sheet, and wrapped the bundle in sturdy chains. Evans slipped on several padlocks and handed Jack the keys. Jack slipped them into his pocket, next to the signed Power of Attorney, and checked his watch. Almost time for first sitting. He had to be there, to be seen in public. He needed witnesses.

Evans rolled her shrouded body onto the gurney and followed Jack into the bedroom, where the emaciated corpse still lay on his bed. The throat had been ripped, the edges ragged and pale. There wasn't much blood left to clean up. Jack had seen worse; he'd done worse.

"Take them both to the ice house. I'll inform the Captain of the deaths. Poor Lady Ambrose, to be taken so...young." He shook his head. "And Lord Sebastian: one dalliance too many. In his exhausted state, the infection took hold quickly." He tapped a fresh cigarillo out of its silver case.

"Put Lady Ambrose in the maid's coffin, box it up and pack well with ice. It should help muffle any sound if she should wake early. The maid will join Bucknall, Lord Sebastian, and the rest of the influenza victims to be cremated on arrival."

"You'll need these." He handed Evans the paperwork. "This allows me to take charge of the suicide's coffin to deliver to the authorities. The Captain was all too grateful I would take charge. He has a schedule to maintain. Unfortunately, both the report, and the body, will be mislaid."

Evans nodded and kicked the gurney into life. Cogs whirred. Small balls of steam puffed across the floor.

Jack returned to the bedroom, caught up the edge of the bedclothes with the spiked end of his walking cane, and flipped them over the corpse. He screwed the silver cap back onto the end of his cane and rested it against the armchair.

"I want everything cleared up before I return from dinner."

"Yes, sir."

Jack donned his dinner jacket and examined himself in the mirror. He wiped a speck of blood from his cheek.

His voyage had been unexpectedly rewarding. Tomorrow he would arrive in Australia ready to begin his final, and most promising, experiments.

Afterword

(Ideas, Jack the Ripper, and how the story evolved.)

James Findlay was first introduced in *Doctor Jack & Other Tales*, the first book of *The Adventures of Viola Stewart*.

If you've already read *Doctor Jack*, the following provides background to the character's origins. For those who haven't read *Doctor Jack*, be warned: there are spoilers ahead.

Character Creation

Almost anything can spark my ideas. Sometimes it's sudden, sometimes several ideas must fall into place before it works. For James Findlay, it was both.

It started with a song: The Who's *Behind Blue Eyes*. It's a hauntingly sad song, written from the point of view of a man shunned and hated. Misunderstood. A villain. The idea of writing from the villain's point of view, the hero of his version of the story, had rolled around my head for a few years. I'm fascinated with how the mind works, why one person becomes a hero, another the 'bad guy'. How is a villain created? Was it nurture or nature? What makes them tick? I was driven by my desire for catharsis. If I understood, then I could forgive. I just had to find the right character.

I wanted my readers to empathise with them – despite knowing they were the villain – even if only for a moment.

Who is James Findlay?

James Findlay was originally just 'Jack'; Jack the Ripper to be precise.

In 1888, speculation about the identity of Jack the Ripper captured the imagination of a terrified society. The Ripper's identity is still unsolved, and still captures our imagination over 160 years later.

In 2014, there was a slew of Ripper documentaries, likely triggered by the publication of a book by Russel Edwards claiming to uncover the real identity of Jack the Ripper. The book centred on new evidence: a silk shawl, bought at an auction in 2007. It was alleged to have been taken from the scene by a policeman, handed down through the family, and eventually returned to the descendants of Catherine Eddowes. Russell claimed recent DNA testing proved it belonged to Catherine Eddowes (linking her descendants to blood stains on the scarf). He also claimed bodily fluids belonged to one of the original Ripper suspects, Aaron Kosminski.

Previously, DNA testing had been done on saliva from a stamp on a letter thought to have been sent by the Ripper (reported to be a hoax by Sir Charles Warren in October 1888) which led to speculation that the Ripper was a woman.

There'd been a female suspect at the time. Even Arthur Conan Doyle had speculated the Ripper could be a woman, possibly a midwife. Inspector Abberline had suggested that the killer had left the scene of the last canonical Ripper murder – that of Mary Kelly – disguised in women's clothing.

Though tantalizing, neither had unbroken, documented 'chain of evidence', so provenance is not proven beyond a doubt. In addition, it was not uncommon in the 19th century, for stamps to be placed on letters by post office staff, many of whom were female.

And now my inner science geek is really showing: testing on the silk shawl was via mitochondrial DNA, which is inherited from the mother. It can't identify a specific individual, but could belong to one of (tens of) thousands of people alive today. Today, it's used to exclude suspects from a pool, not identify an individual suspect.

Who do I think was Jack the Ripper? That is a rabbit hole worthy of an epic Alice of Wonderland tale. Most likely, we'll never know.

Personally, I'm intrigued by Charles Cross. Initially, he seemed an innocent witness, having claimed to discover the body of Mary Ann Nichol (the first canonical Ripper victim) in Buck's Row. Cross called for a passerby Robert Paul to join him to inspect the body. When accounting for foot traffic and constable's routes, it was possible Cross could've been alone with the body for up to nine minutes. This led to later speculation Cross may have interrupted mid-attack.

Both men were running late for work, so told the first policeman they met. Cross left, saying he was wanted by another policeman back in Bucks Row.

He didn't come forward until newspapers reported a second witness discovered the body, and testified under a false name (Cross was his step-father's last name) in court. When giving evidence, he denied mentioning a second constable at the scene. 'Charles Cross' disappeared after the coroner's hearing. It wasn't until 2000, that 'Charles Cross' was found to be an alias. His real name was Charles Allen Lechmere.

His occupation meant blood stains on clothing would not be suspicious. He lived near three of the murder scenes and wasn't working the night of the double (murder) 'event'.

Was Charles Cross, aka Charles Allen Lechmere, the Ripper? There is no conclusive proof he was the Ripper. But there is also no proof to discount him.

Rather than choose an already named suspect, I decided, as it was an alternate history, to create my own fictional Ripper.

James Findlay became an adversary worthy of my existing heroine Viola Stewart, the widowed optician with a penchant for solving murders (*The Adventures of Viola Stewart*).

His character developed as I wrote. He studied in Edinburgh (with Viola Stewart and Henry Collins – more on him later). He was a focused surgeon, if a little macabre in his methods. He's done morally dubious things in his past. James Findlay became an antihero, with many flaws, considering his work beneficial to society, willing to sacrifice individuals for the good of the many. The more I write, the more I learn about him. He's my tool to delve into the psyche of the villain. He helps me explore their motives.

And proved to be the perfect opponent for my feisty heroine Viola…

But had I created a character the reader could identify

with, despite his flaws and psychopathic tendencies? When I received feedback from my editor (thank you Sharon), I got my answer: *For a few seconds I thought, oh poor Jack… then I thought: you bastard.* It was the best feedback I could ask for.

The Many Names of James Findlay

James has assumed many names and personas. After revisiting my research to write Blood Ties, I wondered if Charles Lechmere's use of an alias, and the many possible identities of Jack the Ripper, had led me to the creation of James' cavalier use of aliases and identity theft. Then there was his chosen name: James Findlay. In 2019, the shawl DNA was retested by Australian scientist, Professor Ian Findlay (no relation). Had I plucked the name from my subconscious? To be honest, I'd forgotten the details.

But what about his other names?

The monicker Doctor Jack was a later development (I was a dedicated pantser – writing by the seat of my pants), and was the name given to him by his local Whitechapel patients. In Blood Ties, he introduces himself as Dr Collins, retired police surgeon.

Who is Doctor (Henry) Collins?

If you haven't read *Doctor Jack*, here's a quick explanation. Doctor (Henry) Collins was Viola Stewart's love interest in *The Adventures of Viola Stewart* series. Whether out of jealousy, a way to corrupt the memory of his rival, or a twisted joke, it was a ruse with an added bonus - if James was caught, he could escape and lay the blame on his rival.

Blood Ties.

I spoke before of the sparks for the original concept of James' character and his introduction. *Blood Ties* was originally written for a Canadian steampunk anthology with darker themes. The brief was: a tale of Gaslamp and 'dreadpunk', embracing Victorian gothic, include at least one monstrous or undead creature, with cogs and gears used sparingly, i.e. light on the steampunk.

I wanted to write another James Findlay story, following directly after he boarded ship at the end of *Doctor Jack.* The editor was happy to accept a story with my existing character.

At the beginning of *Blood Ties*, James has fled London on board a ship bound for Australia – partly to avoid capture, and partly to extricate himself from the Men in Grey, who'd been funding his experiments as payment for his services. Does he trust them? No. Does he have regrets? Yes, the biggest having sacrificed one of the only people he's loved to further the Men in Grey's plans. Does he think his actions were wrong? No, he considers them justified.

But what of the plot? What story would enfold on his journey?

More research, and I'd like to thank Trove for the final cog in the machine, as it were. I found an article about an influenza epidemic on board a steamship bound for Adelaide, South Australia. The premise was set: What if the influenza outbreak was a cover up for the dread work of an undead creature? Add a murder, a mystery, a little gothic romance, and betrayal…

Blood Ties was originally published in *Deadsteam II* anthology by Grimmer & Grimmer Books (2021) It is the first in a planned series of shorter and mini adventures of *The James Findlay Journals*. James' experiments also pave the way for a future series mulling in my brain…

Acknowledgements

Blood Ties is set directly after *Doctor Jack* novella originally written and published in 2015, as part of the first book of my first Victorian steampunk mystery series *The Adventures of Viola Stewart*. It was first published in the 2021 *Deadsteam II* anthology published by Grimmer & Grimmer Books.

Thank you to my friends, for their generosity and support and to Bryce Raffle who helped wrangle it into submission for its first outing. Thank you, also, to true crime author and Ripperologist Amanda Howard, who beta read *Doctor Jack,* my first James Findlay novella.

And thank you to my readers who insisted I continue James Findlay's journey.

About the Author

Karen J Carlisle lives in Adelaide with her family and the ghost of her ancient Devon Rex cat. She loves fantasy fiction, gardening, historical re-creation, and steampunk and can often be found plotting fantastical, piratic or airship adventures. Karen has always loved chocolate and rarely refuses a cup of tea. She is not keen on South Australian summers.

www.karenjcarlisle.com

You can support Karen at:
https://www.patreon.com/KarenJCarlisle
https://ko-fi.com/karenjcarlisle

Follow Karen at:
www.goodreads.com/KarenJCarlisle
https://www.instagram.com/karenjcarlisle/
https://www.tiktok.com/@karenjcarlisle
https://www.facebook.com/KarenJCarlisle
https://twitter.com/kjcarlisle

Sign up for Karen's newsletter:
https://karenjcarlisle.com/sign-up-email-list/

Other works by Karen J Carlisle

Available in paperback and eBook:
The Adventures of Viola Stewart series:
Doctor Jack & Other Tales: Journal #1
Eye of the Beholder & Other Tales: Journal #2
The Illusioneer & Other Tales: Journal #3

The Aunt Enid Mysteries
Aunt Enid: Protector Extraordinaire
A Fey Tale

The Department of Curiosities
The Department of Curiosities

Collections
Cogs and Conspiracies: A collection of steampunk short stories

Coming soon
Secrets of the Empire
(Book 2, The Department of Curiosities)

Available as eBooks only:
Short Story Collections
With a Twist of the Nib: For when time is short
Another Twist of the Nib: Shorter Tales with a Darker Twist
Quarantine Reads: Escape to Adventure

The Adventures of Viola Stewart series:
Tomorrow, When I Die: A Christmas Adventure

Mrs Hudson Investigates
Mrs Hudson Investigates
The Case of the Forgotten Letter

www.ingramcontent.com/pod-product-compliance
Lightning Source LLC
Chambersburg PA
CBHW020534120726
47904CB00003B/1071